PALACE
of
BOOKS

To the keepers of our culture—the librarians—and especially to
the Willard Library, with gratitude,
and to Dick Strader, librarian and storyteller

SIMON & SCHUSTER BOOKS FOR YOUNG READERS
An imprint of Simon & Schuster Children's Publishing Division
1230 Avenue of the Americas, New York, New York 10020
© 2023 by Patricia Polacco
Book design by Laurent Linn © 2023 by Simon & Schuster, Inc.
All rights reserved, including the right of reproduction in whole or in part in any form.
SIMON & SCHUSTER BOOKS FOR YOUNG READERS and related marks are trademarks of Simon & Schuster, Inc.
For information about special discounts for bulk purchases, please contact Simon & Schuster Special Sales
at 1-866-506-1949 or business@simonandschuster.com.
The Simon & Schuster Speakers Bureau can bring authors to your live event. For more information or to book an event,
contact the Simon & Schuster Speakers Bureau at 1-866-248-3049 or visit our website at www.simonspeakers.com.
The text for this book was set in PT Serif.
The illustrations for this book were rendered in pencil, marker, and acrylic paint.
Manufactured in China
1022 SCP
First Edition
2 4 6 8 10 9 7 5 3 1
Library of Congress Cataloging-in-Publication Data
Names: Polacco, Patricia, author, illustrator.
Title: Palace of books / Patricia Polacco.
Description: First edition. | New York : Simon & Schuster Books for Young Readers, 2023. | "A Paula Wiseman Book." |
Audience: Ages 4-8. | Audience: Grades 2-3. | Summary: At the public library in her new town, Patricia meets Mrs. Creavy,
an encouraging librarian who introduces Patricia to the books of John James Audubon and helps her become the first
member of the Audubon bird club of Fremont Elementary.
Identifiers: LCCN 2021051943 (print) | LCCN 2021051944 (ebook)
| ISBN 9781534451315 (hardcover) | ISBN 9781534451322 (ebook)
Subjects: CYAC: Libraries—Fiction. | Books and reading—Fiction. | Birds—Fiction. | LCGFT: Picture books.
Classification: LCC PZ7.P75186 Pal 2022 (print) | LCC PZ7.P75186 (ebook) | DDC [E]—dc22
LC record available at https://lccn.loc.gov/2021051943
LC ebook record available at https://lccn.loc.gov/2021051944

PALACE of BOOKS

— Written and illustrated by —

PATRICIA POLACCO

A PAULA WISEMAN BOOK

SIMON & SCHUSTER
BOOKS FOR YOUNG READERS
NEW YORK   LONDON   TORONTO   SYDNEY   NEW DELHI

It was a sunny day. There was a very slight breeze that rustled the leaves in the trees and made waves across our wheat field, like on the surface of lake water. I was sitting on the fender of my grandfather's old tractor. One of my favorite things to do. Grampa was tilling the pasture for one last time. We were all moving away from this place the next day.

Suddenly Grampa made a sharp turn and circled a small spot in the field, only to return to tilling the row.

"Grampa . . . why did you do that?" I asked.

"Because there is a thrasher who has her nest and hatchlings within those grasses. I always protect them and plow around them. She is nesting her babies," he answered.

As I looked at the field, it was dotted with many spots of tall grasses. "Are all of those nests?" I asked him.

He nodded.

My grandfather was a wondrous, kind man who had a deep regard for nature, and certainly for the wild birds that lived on our farm.

My bubbie had passed away that May, and Grampa had sold our farm. He was going to live with Uncle George and Aunt Doris in Indiana.

Momma had rented an apartment in Battle Creek just down the street from the school where she taught. At the school year's end we were moving to California.

"I'm going to miss rides on the tractor, Grampa," I said sadly. "And who will go owling with me this winter? . . . There are owls in Battle Creek, aren't there?" I asked.

"Yes," Grampa said.

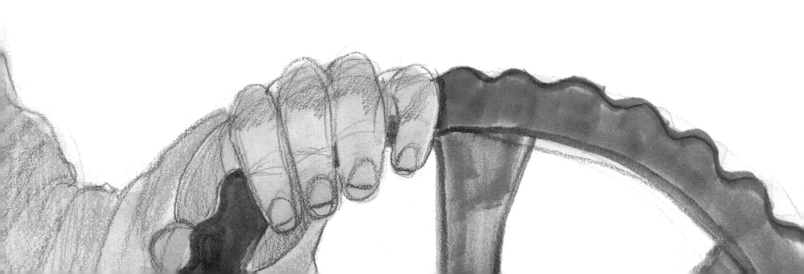

As we got to the barn, I saw swallows diving and circling the sky as they darted into the haymow, only to glide back out, soar up higher than high, and dive again.

Then I heard the rhythmic tapping of a woodpecker as it was pecking for beetles and worms in the bark of one of our many maple trees.

"I'm going to miss Henry crowing in the morning," I whispered as I looked at our chickens scratching and pawing the barnyard with their feet.

Our geese hooted and hissed as we passed them, and our ducks quacked excitedly as we rounded the corner of the coop.

They were ruffling the water in our small duck pond to bring worms up from the bottom. Their bright orange webbed feet patted the wet mud as they circled one another and chattered.

"They are going to be well cared for, Trisha," Grampa reassured me. "The Clarks will care for them just as much as we do," Grampa said as he patted my cheek.

As we sat for the last time in front of our fireplace that night, we just looked at the embers and talked about all the things we loved about being there. . . .

"Grampa, there will be lots of birds in the city, won't there?" I whispered.

"Oh, sweetie, of course. Birds are everywhere. They are the creatures of the air. They fly where they wish," Grampa told me.

We all slept on the floor that night in front of the fire.

The next morning we all rushed around getting ready to leave. I found myself saying goodbye to Bubbie's wallpaper in her room . . . running my hand over the pig stone in the center of the hearth. It was shaped just like a pig! When Uncle George and Aunt Doris got there, we all packed our cars.

Finally we were standing in the expanse of the front yard.

No one could say anything. Then we just took each other's hands and stood in a circle. Then we hugged, kissed, and trundled into our cars.

As we pulled out of the long driveway, I looked back at our house until we rounded the corner that took us onto the county road to the highway.

"We'll see him as often as we like," Momma said as she brushed tears from her eyes.

"Garrett, Indiana, isn't that far from Battle Creek," she went on to say.

But to my brother, Richie, and me, everything we knew was coming to an end.

We watched the movers pack up all of our home piece by piece as we said goodbye to our friends and neighbors.

It wasn't long before we left rolling meadows, tall barns, and thickly wooded lands that were so much a part of my life. I couldn't imagine what it would be like to be anywhere else.

Then looming in the distance I could see tall buildings. All clumped together, they looked like they were leaning on one another. It was Battle Creek!

Finally we were in the middle of the city. All the streets were made of brick!

"This is our street," Momma said as she pulled into a driveway next to a very stately-looking mansion. It was the fanciest house I had ever seen. It had big round pillars in front and a wide porch with statues on it.

"Momma . . . are we going to live in this?" Richie said in astonishment.

"No, this is where our landlady lives. Her name is Marguerite Bowman. . . . We are going to live there!" Momma announced as she gestured at the coach house at the end of the driveway, behind the big main house.

As I looked up and down the street, I saw that all of the houses were fancier than fancy.

But this one had this beautiful little cottage. We would be living there until Momma's teaching job in California next fall.

When Momma unlocked the door, we were greeted by familiar furniture. She'd had the movers pick up our belongings and bring them there a couple of days before. The rest of our things were in a van bound for California.

"Now you two will have to share a room," Momma said as she led us up a few small steps to a landing. "This apartment only has two bedrooms. I took the smaller one, and you two will have the larger one.

"Mrs. Bowman was nice enough to loan me the bunk beds. She even gave me a kitchen table and other things we'll need," Momma said. Then we went downstairs and helped unpack groceries into cupboards.

"Look, Richie," I sang out. "The floors are made out of brick!"

"This used to be the coach house. Buggies were probably kept here, and the horses, too," Momma said as she smiled.

"Well . . . how do you like it?" She beamed.

"We love it, Momma," we both said.

We all unloaded the car and put our things away and hung up things that needed to be in the closet.

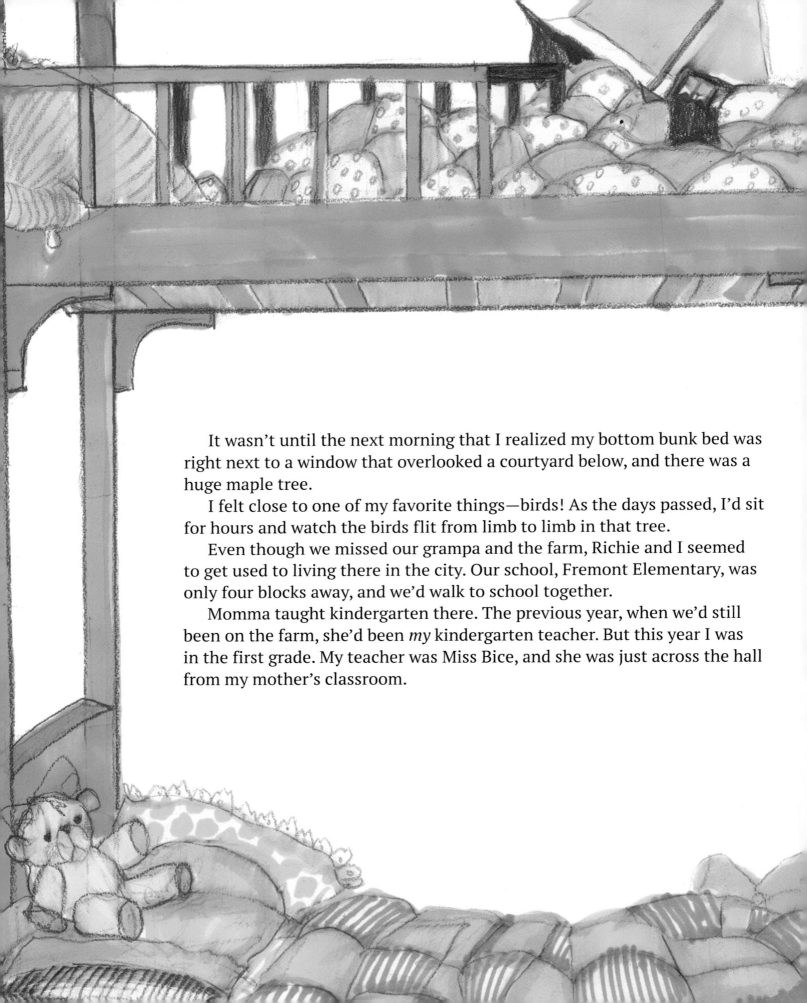

It wasn't until the next morning that I realized my bottom bunk bed was right next to a window that overlooked a courtyard below, and there was a huge maple tree.

I felt close to one of my favorite things—birds! As the days passed, I'd sit for hours and watch the birds flit from limb to limb in that tree.

Even though we missed our grampa and the farm, Richie and I seemed to get used to living there in the city. Our school, Fremont Elementary, was only four blocks away, and we'd walk to school together.

Momma taught kindergarten there. The previous year, when we'd still been on the farm, she'd been *my* kindergarten teacher. But this year I was in the first grade. My teacher was Miss Bice, and she was just across the hall from my mother's classroom.

This year was exciting because Miss Bice took our class out on nature walks in the woods behind the playground of our school.

I loved the woods, and whenever we went there, it was like being back on our farm! And there were so many birds!

Richie joined the Cub Scouts and on some days would stay after school for their pack meetings. On those days I walked home from school alone. I was impressed by all the really big fancy houses that were on the same street as Mrs. Bowman's. One day I went a block out of my way, on a street that took me to the train depot. As I turned up the brick street to our house, there were several enormous buildings before the fancy houses.

WILLARD
LIBRARY

One building fascinated me. It was tall and stately. It had giant pillars all along the front of it, on a porch that had millions of steps up to it. On each side of the steps there was a scary-looking lion on a huge pedestal.

Their eyes seemed to be looking to a far-off place, but there were times when I felt they were looking right at me!

That night at dinner I asked my mother what that fancy building was.

"Oh, sweetie, that's the public library," she answered as she spooned a bowl of soup for me.

"A library!" I chirped. "You mean they have a whole big building that is only for books?" I exclaimed. "It looks like a palace where a king or queen would live!"

Grampa had books, and so did Momma, but they kept them on shelves in the living room.

"Oh, Trisha, they have thousands of volumes in a library," Momma went on.

"Why are they there?" I asked.

"I imagine so people can go in and read them," Momma answered.

"You mean that I can go into that palace?" I crowed.

"Of course you can. Libraries are places that lend their books out so people can borrow them and take them home," Momma said matter-of-factly.

"To keep?" I asked.

"Oh, no," Momma answered. "No, they are only lent out. Usually for a week at a time. Then when the patron is finished reading or looking at them, the person brings the books back to the library so someone else can see those books."

"Then can the person borrow more of them?" I trumpeted.

"Yes!" Momma insisted as she got up to do the dishes.

"Tomorrow on my way home I want to go visit that palace!" I announced.

Momma said I could as long as I was home before four o'clock.

The next morning Miss Bice took my class out on a nature walk.

When all the other kids were running about, I scanned the ground, looking for something my grampa had showed me many times.

I found one, picked it up, and examined it closely.

Some of the other kids and Miss Bice came over to me.

"What is that?" one of the kids asked.

"It's an owl pellet. When an owl eats a mouse, she swallows it whole. Then her stomach puts all the fur and bones into a little package, and she throws it up," I answered with authority.

"EEEEEEEOOOOOOOOOO," they hollered, and backed away.

"If you cut it open, you can see the bones and fur," I informed them, trying to convince them not to recoil.

"Patricia," Miss Bice whispered, "how wonderfully interesting. We shall take this in and put it in our science corner...." She smiled as she took it and put it into her pocket.

"And do you see that small basket hanging from the limb way up there? That is the nest of a Baltimore oriole, one of the only birds that builds a hanging basket for a nest," I said as I pointed it out to Miss Bice.

"And there's a blue jay, right there near that robin," I said.

"It seems like you know your birds, Patricia," Miss Bice exclaimed.

"Yeah. On our farm my grampa and I used to go bird-watching.... That oriole really isn't supposed to be here. Michigan is too far away from Maryland...." My voice trailed off.

I was the new kid, and I sensed that the other kids hadn't met anyone like me, so I didn't say any more.

That afternoon after school I walked very briskly to the grand palace for books! I was so excited about going inside. But when I got there, those lions seemed to be looking right at me! The steps seemed to go on and on . . . FOREVER!

When I finally got to the top, I was on an entry porch. There were doors so tall and thick that I could hardly open them. They were heavy!

When I got inside, there was a very tall and wide man who seemed to be guarding the door! He motioned me inside.

As I walked through a high archway, I found myself standing on a highly polished marble floor. It was so shiny that I could see myself when I looked down. Then as I walked in, I saw a round dome that was right in the middle of the ceiling. Underneath it was a row of desks behind a carved wood wall.

The wood wall was in the shape of a circle. There was a sign in front of it, but I hadn't learned to read yet, so I didn't know what the sign said.

I could see the top of a lady's head. She was just answering the phone, so I waited until she noticed me.

"Yes, dear. How can I help you today?" she finally said politely.

She had bright red hair, just like my brother, and she wore big glasses with wire rims. She had a very friendly smile.

I just looked at her. . . . I didn't know what to say.

"The children's room is just past the rotunda and to your left, dear," she whispered as she pointed at another archway.

BOOK RETURN

I backed away from the desks and just started walking around and looking. I looped in and out of the high shelves of books that circled the rotunda. Then I saw a group of books that all had rich-looking covers. They were wider and taller than most books. So I pulled one of them from the shelf. It fell with a slap and echoed into the main room. I sat down on the floor and pulled the very heavy book into my lap and opened it.

I caught my breath. It had beautiful color pictures of paintings on each page. With every turn of the page the pictures were more and more glorious! Someday I wanted to paint and draw exactly like these artists!

"This is the one I want to borrow," I whispered to myself.

I struggled to my feet, picked up the huge book, and started to make my way to the doors.

"Oh, sweetie," the red-haired woman called out.

She trotted from behind the desks directly over to me. Her heels made a loud clicking sound on the marble floor. All the people who were sitting at long tables with green reading lamps looked up . . . right at me!

"Honey, where are you going with that volume?" she whispered.

"I'm borrowing it! My momma said that I can borrow books from here!" I chirped.

The redheaded lady knelt down and was eye to eye with me. She smiled warmly so I knew I wasn't in any kind of trouble.

"Of course the books in this library are for people to borrow, but unfortunately, you have a very valuable art book that is from our private collection and is not meant to be borrowed," she whispered as she took it into her arms.

She could see how disappointed and embarrassed I was.

"But, darlin', you can come here at any time and look at them as much as you want," she reassured me as she patted my cheek.

"Is your mother here with you?" she asked.

"No, she's still at school. . . . Fremont. . . . She's a teacher. I'm supposed to be home by four," I whispered.

"Do you live nearby?" she asked.

"We live in Mrs. Bowman's coach house," I answered.

"Marguerite Bowman. We know her very well!" the redheaded lady said. "What is your name?" she asked me.

"Patricia. . . . Patricia Barber," I answered.

"Well, Marguerite Bowman's house is only a few houses away. Come in tomorrow and bring your mother. I'll arrange for you to get a library card," she said warmly.

"A library card?" I questioned.

"Yes, dear. You need one in order to remove and borrow a book from the library. We have hundreds of books just for you in the children's room."

I didn't want to go to the children's room. I wanted to look at all the art books. I loved to draw and paint. Someday I wanted to be a great artist. So THOSE were the books I wanted to see!

"Bring your mother tomorrow, and I'll have a library card just for you!"

I smiled at her and waved as I walked toward the door.

"Just ask for me, sweetie. My name is Mrs. Creavy," she called out as I left.

The next morning in class Miss Bice was passing out string necklaces with small plastic circles strung on them. They were all green.

"Now, my dears, you are all members of the green-circle reading club. Today is the first day that you are going to learn to read!" she announced as she walked around the room, slipping the strings over our heads.

"As you advance and learn, you will get circles of a different color. The more you read . . . then you get a different color!" she said, and smiled.

As time passed, some of the kids had yellow circles, some had red circles, some had blue. But I stayed in the green-circle group. Pretty soon I was the only one! Reading was so hard for me. I couldn't understand why, but it was! The one thing I could do really well was draw! Miss Bice always had me do the drawings for any class report. And my artwork was hanging all over the room. Momma had gotten my library card for me, and almost every day after school I'd go to the library and lie on the floor and look at those beautiful art books.

Momma and Mrs. Creavy had become friends. And Mrs. Creavy was a friend of mine, too.

I was Miss Bice's star on the nature walks. It got so that I could just about tell them what every bird we saw was!

One day Miss Bice announced to our class that every classroom at our school was going to have an open house on the night of the parents' visit to the school.

And we all needed to think about a theme.

That day after school when I got to the library, I told Mrs. Creavy about our open house. And that each kid was to think about a theme.

"What would you choose for a theme, Patricia?" Mrs. Creavy asked me.

"Birds!" I answered without hesitation.

"Birds," Mrs. Creavy said thoughtfully.

"I've been doing drawings of birds ever since we moved here. A mother robin has built a nest outside my window, and I draw her almost every day. . . ."

"Patricia, I think that it is time for you to see something very special here at the library. The public is not allowed to visit this room, but I think that you are the perfect person to take there. . . . Come with me, dear," Mrs. Creavy said with a flourish of her arms.

She took me onto the elevator, and we went as far as it could go. Then we got off and went up two more sets of stairs . . . then to a place where there was a spiral set of metal stairs.

As we climbed them, I could see that the floor of this upper room was glass bricks. The light from the floor beneath shone through them, giving them a feeling of being in a heavenly place.

"Sit right down here, sweetie," Mrs. Creavy whispered. Then she went to a door with a wheel on it and started cranking it. The thick door opened and she went in.

"These are the stacks, Patricia . . . a place where the most valued volumes are kept."

With that, she walked out with a leather-bound book that was as big as she was. She placed it on a table and put on white gloves. She had some for me, too.

"What you are about to see in these great big editions are the paintings of John James Audubon! Not only a lover of nature but also one of the finest watercolorists in the world."

She opened the book, and I gasped at the sight of what I beheld. PAINTINGS OF BIRDS! Each page had a picture that was more beautiful or exciting than the previous one. Every feather, every detail, re-created in its perfection. I started to cry. I had never seen anything more beautiful than this! EVER IN MY LIFE!

When I got home, I was thinking of what Mrs. Creavy told me.
"John James Audubon was a naturalist and also an artist. . . . Do you know that there are Audubon bird clubs and societies all over the world because of his studies and paintings?"

I wanted to belong to that. And she told me about the Kellogg Bird Sanctuary that was just down the road next to the Museum of Natural History. Mrs. Creavy said that almost every bird was there and that she could get tickets, maybe enough for my entire class.

I worked on my bird paintings until it was time for bed.

When I went to class the next day, I brought all the drawings of birds that I had ever done. Miss Bice and my whole class were astonished!

"I think our theme should be all about birds," Lennie Hummer piped up.

"Me too!" Julia Borden echoed.

Pretty soon the whole class voted and decided that birds would be our theme for the open house!

"And Trisha's drawings should be up everywhere!" Nancy Havens added.

"And look," I announced. "Mrs. Creavy at the library has given us all tickets to go to the Kellogg Bird Sanctuary!"

Later at the art show, I thanked Mrs. Creavy and told her how excited the class was when I told them the whole class was going to the Bird Sanctuary.

The next week Miss Bice organized a field trip to the sanctuary. I hadn't known that there was such a place, where beautiful birds could live free from harm, and people could visit them. I had never seen so many different kinds of birds in one place. I was in heaven!

As soon as we got back to school, my whole class busied ourselves making a bird sanctuary of our own. We studied pictures of birds and drew them. We made birds by covering light bulbs with tissue paper and hanging them from the ceiling. We thatched nests and brought small branches and attached them to our walls. Pretty soon our room looked like a forest, with every kind of bird resting on branches. Some were papier-mâché, some were tissue over paper bags, and some were drawings.

When we had completed our beautiful bird sanctuary, our class invited Mrs. Creavy to come see what we had done. Momma was invited too. All she had to do was come across the hall from her room.

When Mrs. Creavy arrived, a very official-looking man was with her. After they had inspected every inch of our bird sanctuary, Mrs. Creavy announced to our class that the man with her was Mr. Bledsoe, the Michigan state chairman of the Audubon bird clubs of America.

"Children, with the permission of your principal and your school, I have come to offer all of you memberships in the Audubon bird club, in recognition of all your fine work!" he sang out.

Then he looked at me.

"And this, my dear, is for you," he said as he bent down and pinned a small badge onto my dress. "You, Patricia, are officially the first member of the Audubon bird club of Fremont Elementary!" He beamed.

I was so proud. Maybe I didn't have any more than a green circle for reading, but I had earned THIS! It was robin's-egg blue and had a picture of a robin on it.

All the kids cheered, and Momma and Mrs. Creavy and Miss Bice had tears in their eyes.

Our open house was a huge success. Mr. Thomas, our principal, invited the board of education to come see our bird sanctuary. We were featured in the paper. There were lots of pictures!

And even though I would be leaving Battle Creek for California at the end of the school year, I felt like I had started something very special at Fremont Elementary School.

AUTHOR'S NOTE

The Audubon bird club lasted at Fremont Elementary School for the next sixty years! The school was closed in 2016 but later reopened. But to this day I'm still proud of what we did.

To think that none of it would have happened if I had not discovered the wonder of that magnificent palace of books . . . and Mrs. Creavy, of course. . . . It was she who took me into the stacks and introduced me to Audubon and his glorious paintings!

Reading remained very difficult for me, however. I learned in later years that I have dyslexia; dysnomia, which means I have trouble remembering letters and numbers; dysgraphia; and a failure of sensory integration. I shall remember with gratitude and sincere measure the heart of that wondrous librarian, Mrs. Creavy, as long as I live! It was she who made it her business to deliver those amazing books into my gaze. She brought a beauty into my life that still resonates, with an appreciation of color, shape, design, and composition. I not only memorized many species of birds but also learned to identify the works of hundreds of artists because of her. That generous single act of sharing the beauty that was within those books assured my future as an artist . . . an author . . . and an amateur ornithologist.

Thank you, Mrs. Creavy . . . wherever you are.

I still have my Audubon bird club pin that was placed on my chest over sixty years ago!

The Willard Library and Patricia's library card.

Expires April 19 1949

Barber, Patricia

173 Capital Ave. NE
Battle Creek, Mich.
is responsible for all use made of this card

Willard Library
Battle Creek, Mich.

Nº 123456

If card is lost it will be replaced on payment of ten cents.

THIS CARD MUST BE PRESENTED
EACH TIME A BOOK IS BORROWED

Ⓖ Pat. Re. 20344